CONTENTS

CAST LIST

2 Narrators	*On stage, observing and commentating, throughout most of the performance*
3 Guards	*1 with speaking part*
King Darius	*A little unsure of his own mind, but with authority and stature*
Governors*	*4 with speaking parts*
Calvinus	*Fashion stylist to the King*
Kleinius	*Calvinus' partner in fashion crime*
Chariot spotters*	*As 'nerdy' as you dare. 2 with speaking parts*
French chef	*Perhaps with chef's hat, checked trousers, curly moustache and string of onions!*
2 crèche girls	*A little giggly when in Daniel's company*
Girl	*One of courtiers with plenty of adoration for Daniel*
Angels*	*Graceful and gentle.*

Hebrew captives*

Daniel	*Popular and charismatic leading character*
Shadrach	*Daniel's friend*
Meshach	*Daniel's friend*
Abednego	*Daniel's friend*

6 more with speaking parts

Lions and trainers*

Nibbler	*Very hungry lion – only one line to 'growl'*
Nora	*Lion trainer*
Annie	*Lion trainer*

At least 3 more lions

Non-speaking parts

Courtiers*	*Includes servants with fruit, drinks etc, entertainers (brightly dressed), possibly some holding large feather fans. All ready to serve the King at any given moment!*
Servant girl	*Slightly clumsy*
Conscience*	*This group sing song 5 – Jealousy And Hatred. Could double as angels*
Jealousy and hatred*	*Dancers in Jealousy And Hatred song.*
Royal dancers*	*Could double as Conscience, Angels, and/or J&H dancers*

* These groups can include as many children as required, in non-speaking parts

DANIEL
A HARD ACT TO SWALLOW

> The needs of schools vary considerably depending upon a number of factors ranging from their size to the demographic composition of their catchments. What is appropriate for one school may therefore not be appropriate for another. With this in mind, for the purposes of staging this musical, Out of the Ark Music grants schools the right to adapt the script as the local situation dictates. The only stipulation is that the overall structure and storyline of the script be retained.

The background should suggest a hot, Eastern country. There could be a banner hung, 'Welcome to Babylon!' Two narrators enter and stand centre stage.

Narrator 1	*(Facing audience)* Have you ever heard the saying that bad news travels fast?
Narrator 2	Yes! But not the bad news we're going to share with you now. That's taken over two and a half thousand years to reach you today!
Narrator 1	Mind you, there probably weren't so many leaks to the press in those days…
Narrator 2	Ha ha! Look, why don't I just spit it out?
Narrator 1	Go on then… but mind the people in the front row!
Narrator 2	*(Dramatically – telling an adventure story. Narrator 1 reacts)* A long, long, long time ago, Jerusalem was captured by the King of Babylon! And do you know what this mighty king did with the Hebrew captives? Did he chop all their heads off? No! Did he sell them all as slaves? No! He took all the best ones to his own country, all the nobles and intellectuals.
Narrator 1	The really clever people like ……………………………… *(name of head).*
Narrator 2	That's right! He wanted to bring the best to Babylon, but they weren't too happy about it.

Hebrews enter in an orderly way, suggesting prisoners; dragging their feet and looking very woebegone. Some of them carry packages/baggage.

Narrator 2	Look! Here they come! The Hebrew exiles. They're sad and homesick; lonely and confused. They may never see their homes and families again!
Narrator 1	Just like this audience if you don't hurry up! *(Pulls Narrator 2 to the side)* Let's stand here out of the way. The show must go on!
Hebrew 1	I hate it here. Everything smells strange.
Hebrew 2	*(Indicating audience)* And look at the people!
Hebrew 3	Why did we have to come here?
Hebrew 4	Yeah! We want to go home!
Hebrew 5	Why couldn't they have just left us in our own land?
Hebrew 6	We'll always be strangers here. We'll never fit in.
Hebrew 1	Who wants to fit in here? I wanna go back!

All	Yeah. We all wanna go back!
Song 1	**WANNA GO BACK**
Daniel	I know how you feel but we can't go home. We're stuck here now so we might as well make the best of it. Maybe it won't be so bad...
Shadrach	Daniel's right. We have to look on the bright side.
Hebrew 5	There is no bright side.
Hebrew 7	Even God's forgotten about us!
Meshach	Never! Wherever we are, He is with us!
Hebrew 6	All I know is I'll never see my little house again.
Daniel	All I know is that God's still got His eye on us and He knows what He's doing. We have to trust Him.
Hebrew 4	It's all right for you, Daniel. You're young and full of life. Some of us are old and tired...
Daniel	Hey! We're in this together! Let me carry that for you. *(He takes baggage)*
Enter Guard.	
Guard	Come on you lot. Let's get moving. To the palace, quick smart! Off you go! Let's be 'avin you!
Hebrew 4	Letsby Avenue! I thought the palace was on the High Street.
Daniel	*(Laughing)* That's the spirit!

All exit except Narrators, who move back to the centre.

Narrator 2	Now that is a man to watch.
Narrator 1	Who, the bossy guard?
Narrator 2	No! Daniel.
Narrator 1	Why's that then?
Narrator 2	Because he's gonna get to the top of the tree, climb up the ladder so quickly... be such a high flier...
Narrator 1	What is he? Spiderman?
Narrator 2	No, just someone who'll stand up and be counted. He stands out from the crowd because of his natural charm and intelligence, his wit and good looks. Remind you of anyone? *(Thinking him/herself)*
Narrator 1	Oh yeah! Mr/s .... *(Teacher, helper etc)*.
Narrator 2	Huh! Look why don't we just go over to the palace and you'll see what I mean.

Narrators move to side. Palace scene is set. It needs to be busy and colourful. Courtiers enter, some wearing lots of jewellery; some are servants carrying bowls of fruit, titbits, etc. There are a couple of guards. A throne is placed in the centre. All bow as King Darius enters wearing crown. He sits on the throne

Narrator 1	That's Darius, the King.
Narrator 2	I can see that! The crown's a bit of a giveaway!

Governors enter leading Daniel and friends.

Narrator 1	Look! Here comes Daniel. And that's Meshach on the left, Abednego just coming up on the right, and now Shadrach sneaking through on the outside. They're looking good...
Narrator 2	This isn't a chariot race you know!
Governor 1	*(To Daniel and friends)* You may be the cream of the Hebrew crop, but just stand over there boys. Watch and learn.

Daniel and friends stand to one side. Governors gather either side of throne.

Governor 4	Your Wonderfulness!
Governor 3	Your Splendidness!
Governor 1	Your Majesty! That crown looks marvellous on you. It could have been made for you!
Darius	It was.
Governor 2	But of course, your Braininess. There is no-one like you in the whole universe!
Governor 1	You are among the Gods themselves!
Governor 3	Three cheers for King Darius the Magnificent!
All	Hip, hip hooray, etc.

Song 2   **BABYLON**

At end of song the royal designers enter.

Governor 2	The royal designers are here your Majesty. Calvinus and Kleinius.
Darius	Let them come forward.

Governor 2 signals them forward. Everybody gathers round.

Calvinus	King Darius, just look what we've got for you! This will really bring out the colour of your eyes. Now let's just check the size. *(Takes out tape measure and measures)* As I thought, practically perfect in every way!
Kleinius	You'll find it's not just this season, it's next season too, and maybe a few seasons after that! It's so fabulous! It's the new black!

They bring out a hideous, very bright garment and hold it against Darius.

Calvinus	Yes! I knew it! Didn't I tell you it would say 'King!'?
Kleinius	It brings tears to my eyes! *(Court all clap, mutter splendid, marvellous, etc)*

Daniel	*(Moving forward)* Brings tears to your eyes? Tears of laughter you mean! It's certainly saying something... and very loud! All it says to me is, 'You must be joking!'

Everyone gasps and takes a step backwards.

Abednego	Daniel! Be careful what you say.
Daniel	*(Bowing to Darius)* I'm sorry, your Majesty, but I don't think it's very nice to let someone walk round looking like last week's washing. It does nothing for you. It's shapeless and if you ask me the colour/s make you look pale and ill.
Governor 2	Well nobody <u>did</u> ask you. How dare you! You... you... cheeky monkey!! Guards!
Darius	*(Standing up)* Wait! This young man interests me. *(To Daniel)* And I think you're right. It's horrible. *(Court all nod. To the shocked Calvinus and Kleinius...)* You two had better take this and get out quickly before I feed you to the lions! *(Calvinus and Kleinius exit)* Now, <u>you</u>... er...?
Daniel	Daniel, your Majesty
Darius	Right. Daniel. You sit here by me. *(Signals for chair)* I'd like to have your opinion about a few other matters.

Chair is placed on Darius' left. Daniel sits. Governors huddle together in twos or threes and mutter.

Narrator 1	See what I mean. Daniel's already the King's right hand man!
Narrator 2	Left hand man you mean.
Narrator 1	Eh?
Narrator 2	Well. Look, he's sitting on the King's left.
Narrator 1	Did anyone ever tell you, you are <u>really</u> irritating!
Narrator 2	Yeah!
Darius	The Governors have suggested having a statue built of me. *(Everyone claps. Governors bow)* Daniel, perhaps you could help me decide on a suitable pose?
Governor 1	We've done some sketches your Majesty. I think this is the best. It shows your Gloriousness surrounded by chests of gold and precious stones, holding a golden sword as a symbol of your power.

Governor 1 looks around at the other governors who give him thumbs up. They all look very smug. Darius looks to Daniel, who shakes his head.

Daniel	Too showy.
Governor 2	*(Getting a 2nd sketch)* Well, this one depicts your Majesty as a great hunter with his lions - reminding everyone that if they don't do as they're told, they'll be coming to the palace for dinner. In fact, they'll <u>be</u> the dinner. *(All laugh)*
Daniel	Too gory.

Governor 3	(Angrily) Well what would you suggest, Mr Smarty… Daniel?
Daniel	If I were a king…
Governor 4	Which you're not!
Daniel	…I'd want people to feel safe - like they could really trust me. I'd want my subjects to know I cared about them…
Governors	Huh!
Darius	Go on!
Daniel	…So I think your statue should be of a father figure… surrounded by children, perhaps with one or two on your knee. That's what I call a real king.

Governors laugh heartily and encourage others to do the same.

Darius	That is an excellent idea! (To governors) See to it. A drink to celebrate!

Servant girl brings drink. She trips up on the way. Governors and court gasp!

Governor 1	Stupid girl!
Governor 2	Clumsy oaf!
Governor 3	You'll pay for that!

Girl looks terrified. Daniel goes over and helps her up.

Daniel	(Cheerily) Enjoy your trip? I'm always doing things like that.
Darius	Don't worry about the drink, there's plenty more where that came from.

Girl exits. The King and Daniel drink and eat. Courtiers chat in small groups. Governors move to front.

Governor 2	King Darius really seems to like that young fool.
Governor 3	Before you know it, he'll have taken over.
Governor 1	I can't understand it. He's bright, friendly and he tells the truth! What on earth does the King see in him?
Song 3	**HOW DO YOU DO IT?**

During song Daniel and Darius move amongst groups, shaking hands, etc.

Darius	Now, Daniel, do you play chess?
Daniel	I love it, your Majesty.
Darius	Excellent! Come on then. (Signals to servant who brings on chess game)
Governor 1	I bet he doesn't even let the King win. We always let him win.
Governor 2	Actually, he always did win anyway!
Governor 1	Be quiet, I'm trying to think.

Governor 3	That would be a first.
Governor 1	He seems too good to be true. He must have a weak spot...
Governor 2	If anyone can find it, you can.
Governor 1	Come on. We've got some plans to make.

Governors exit. Darius and Daniel move to front and shake hands.

Darius	Well done Daniel! I haven't enjoyed a chess game as much in ages. How about chequers now? *(They move back and continue to play)*
Narrator 1	See, I told you he was one to watch.
Narrator 2	Ah... but is he really all he seems? Maybe underneath he's not so nice.
Narrator 1	You can't use that word! Mr/s .... will kill you! Try affable, sincere, er...
Narrator 2	Maybe underneath he's not so <u>pleasant</u>! Why don't we go and watch him while he's alone? He won't be on his best behaviour then.
Narrator 1	Good idea. *(They begin to exit)*

Group of people walk past wearing anoraks and carrying clipboards.

Narrator 2	Who are they?
Narrator 1	Ah, they're the chariot spotters. Here <u>every</u> week, <u>same</u> time.
Chariot Sp 1	Did you see that? It was a BN29!
Chariot Sp 2	Never! It was a BN27a. I'd swear to it!
Chariot Sp 1	You can't swear here! This is a school production!

All exit. The stage is cleared. Governors enter.

Song 4   SO STUCK UP

All exit at end of song.

Enter Daniel carrying a chair. He sets it front of stage, kneels up on it, facing audience, and mimes opening window in front of him. Narrators also enter. They stand at the side.

Daniel	Thank you Lord that you're with me wherever I go. Even in a foreign land, I can never be out of your sight! Thank you for all my new friends and for King Darius who's been so kind to me! Please help me to be a good subject. Amen.

A knock is heard. Governors enter.

Governor 1	Ah, Daniel. We couldn't help overhearing.
Narrator 1	*(Loudly)* Not with a <u>glass</u> held to the door you couldn't!
Narrator 2	Shhh!
Governor 2	May we ask, to which of the Gods were you praying? We have so many!

Daniel	Yes. But I believe there is only one true God.
Governor 3	Have you got a statue of Him that we could see?
Daniel	Oh no! He's a living God. He's not made of wood or stone.
Governor 1	Really! So he's like a king? A king like Darius?
Daniel	Sort of. But He's not a king of any earthly kingdom. He's King of the whole world!
Governor 2	And you pray to Him every day?
Daniel	That's right. Without fail. I don't know what I'd do without Him.
Governor 1	Right then. Well, we'll leave you to it. Goodbye.
Daniel	Goodbye. Do drop in again.
Governor 3	Don't worry, we will.
Narrator 1	Don't trust them, Daniel.
Daniel	Oh, I don't. *(Waves to governors as they move to back of stage)*
Narrator 2	Did he just talk to you? He's not supposed to do that is he?
Narrator 1	No; but I told you he was different.

Enter French Chef carrying pan and spoon.

Chef	Daniel! Could you just taste zis and zee what you zink?
Daniel	*(Taking a spoonful)* Delicious! Maybe just a pinch of salt… and a little oregano.
Chef	You are a genius! Oregano! Why did I not zink of zat?

As chef exits, 2 or 3 girls enter.

Girl 1	Daniel, could you come to the crèche again later…?
Girl 2	…the little ones really love your stories!
Daniel	Love to!
Girls	Bye then.
Daniel	*(Bowing)* Au revoir, ladies.

They run off, giggling. Daniel exits, taking chair. Governors move forward.

Governor 1	What a creep! I'd like to take out his entrails and knit them into a… a… *(thinks)* tea cosy!
Governor 2	I'd like to pop out his eyeballs and use them to play snooker.
Governor 3	Not much of a game with only two balls.
Governor 2	Shut up or I'll use your eyeballs as well!

Governor 3	I was only saying…
Governor 4	I want to shave off all his hair and use his head as a cotton bud!
Governor 1	Who does he think he is? I hate him! I hate him, I hate him!!

Song 5   **JEALOUSY AND HATRED**

Governors stand in a row, thinking. 'Conscience' people enter, ready to sing.' Jealousy and Hatred' people enter opposite side. During the song J and H people dance around the governors, perhaps using green/red ribbons or a net to ensnare the governors at end of song. Alternatively, J and H could act as puppeteers, standing behind the governors and controlling first one arm, then two etc., in time with music. By the end the governors are totally controlled/trapped. At end of song J & H/Conscience exit.

Governor 2	*(Beginning to pace)* He's got to go! It's just a matter of time. Let's think how we can ruin him. We'll see him torn apart by the lions yet. He doesn't know who he's messing with!
Governor 3	Yeah! We're not going to sit back and let him ruin everything for us.
Governor 2	Not a jumped up little twerp like that.
Governor 1	A nobody!
Governor 4	Just 'cos he's intelligent, charming and… *(as if it's a horrible taste)* honest.

They walk around in 'thinking' mode.

Narrator 1	I don't think they like Daniel very much.
Narrator 2	They're jealous because <u>everybody</u> likes him and <u>nobody</u> likes them.
Narrator 1	Why don't <u>they</u> just try being friendly and kind?
Narrator 2	Some people would rather blame someone else than change themselves.
Narrator 1	That's a bit deep for you.
Narrator 2	I'm not just a pretty face you know.
Governor 1	*(Stopping suddenly)* By George! I think I've got it!
Governor 3	Well don't give it to us!
Governor 1	We just need to work out the details. *(Thoughtfully)* Something to do with his praying. We'll catch him out somehow… Yes! We'll set a trap.

Song 6   **LET'S TRAP HIM**

Governor 1	*(Very excited)* The law! The law!
Governor 2	Where? I don't see any police.
Governor 1	The law of the Medes and the Persians.
Governor 3	Oh yes! *(Puzzled)* What about it?
Governor 1	If King Darius signs a law, even <u>Daniel</u> has to obey it, right?

Governors	Right.
Governor 1	So, we get him to sign a law which says that nobody can pray to <u>anybody</u> but King Darius for 30 days... or *(mimes roaring lions then slitting throat)*.
Governor 4	*(Slowly)* OK... and...?
Governor 1	Do I have to spell it out?
Governor 2	No! Just tell us what it begins with. How many syllables?
Governor 1	*(As if explaining to young children)* If Daniel keeps praying to his God, Darius won't have any choice but to feed him to the lions!
Governor 3	Hey. That's not a bad plan.
Governor 2	It is! It's <u>wicked</u>! Let's do it!
Governor 1	We just need to make sure Daniel is kept out of the way, so he can't interfere.

Daniel enters and walks slowly across the stage reading something. Governor 1 thinks, then quickly comes up with an idea.

Governor 1	Ah Daniel, just the man! We've decided to throw a banquet in the King's honour tonight and thought you might be willing to help us.
Daniel	Of course.
Governor 2	Excellent! You see, we thought you could teach our royal dancers some of the moves from your country. It may help some of the Hebrews feel less homesick.
Daniel	That's really thoughtful. Of course I'd love to help. Just point me in the right direction.
Governor 1	Follow me. The dance studio's this way...

Daniel and Governor 1 exit.

Narrator 1	To the lion's den! That's where they'd <u>like</u> to see you heading.
Narrator 2	Don't worry. Daniel's too clever to be caught out by this lot. Just you wait.

Enter Darius. Governor 1 re-enters carrying clipboard.

Governor 2	Your Roseyscentedness! We are so sorry to trouble you with trifles but there are some documents here needing your signature. Just run of the mill stuff...
Governor 3	Water rates, chariot tax and insurance; bill to ban school holidays; law of the Medes and Persians...
Darius	Law? What law?
Governor 3	Well, it's a bit embarrassing really. We thought that, as you're such a special king, it would be an excellent idea to pass a law stating that <u>no-one </u>should pray to anyone but <u>you</u> for the next thirty days... or they join the lions in their den. It's only because we think you're worth it!
Darius	Oh well, I'm flattered. But I don't think...

Governor 1	We believe it's what the people want, your Majesty. And you have to give the people what they want. (He hands clipboard to Darius)
Darius	Oh well then, I don't suppose it can do any harm. Thirty days you say?
Governor 2	A mere month. It hardly reflects what you deserve but it'll do the trick. I mean it's a heartfelt token of our esteem for you.
Darius	All right, there you are. *(Signs. Hand clipboard back)*

All except Narrators exit.

Narrator 1	This is not looking good. Daniel could get into real trouble!
Narrator 2	Let's just keep our fingers crossed. Everything crossed in fact! Not your eyes dummy! If the wind changes, you'll get stuck!

Daniel and Meshach enter.

Meshach	Have you heard about the new law? We'll have to be careful in future when we pray.
Daniel	My praying doesn't hurt anyone. Why should I feel like a criminal when I'm only doing what I know is right!
Meshach	Because it could kill you! Those governors are just waiting for any excuse to feed you to the lions!
Daniel	That'd be better than being bullied into hiding, and acting as if praying to God is something to be ashamed of!
Meshach	Just be careful, that's all.
Daniel	Don't worry about me. I'm not very tasty anyway!
Meshach	That's not what the servant girls say!

Song 7   **KEEP ON TRUSTING**

Daniel and Meshach exit. Darius and Governors enter.

Darius	Has anyone seen Daniel?
Governor 3	I think I saw him going back to his room just a moment ago. Shall we go and catch him up? Such a jolly fellow. Wonderful company.

They walk round the stage as Daniel appears kneeling on a chair as if praying near a window as before.

Daniel	Lord God, I'm so glad you're my Father and that you care for me so much. Thank you for giving me all I need. I pray that you'll bless the governors and help them to appreciate all they've got, and not to be so...
Governor 2	*(Very loudly; interrupting)* What's that I hear? Someone <u>praying</u>? And not to <u>you</u>!
Darius	*(Aware of Daniel's praying)* I don't hear anything! Come on, let's go back to the palace.
Governor 1	I'm certain I heard somebody praying.

Darius	You've got a vivid imagination! Now, back to the palace!
Daniel	Oh, wonderful God, who is like no other, I just want to say that you are the only God and I worship you.
Governor 2	Oh <u>no</u>! It's <u>Daniel</u>! And he's praying to his own God! You know what this means...
Darius	Why don't we just pretend we didn't hear anything? No-one will ever know.
Narrators	We won't tell!
Governor 2	If only that were possible, your Majesty. But then we would be pretending that <u>we</u> didn't have to obey the laws we make <u>ourselves</u>... and that wouldn't be fair would it? No, I'm afraid we'll just have to do without Daniel's wit and charm. So sad! *(Governors each get out a handkerchief and wipe their eyes. To Darius)* Don't you worry, I'll make the necessary arrangements. Guards!

Very sadly, Darius exits with other governors. 2 guards appear and Governor 1 sends them to get Daniel and drag him off.

Governor 1	*(As he leaves the stage)* Yess!!! Result!!

Guards bring on Daniel and mime locking him in the lions' den. Darius enters and stands on the other side of the stage. He paces around, looking distressed.

Daniel	*(Looking upwards)* Oh Lord. I don't understand why this has happened, but I know I can still trust you to do what's best.
Narrator 1	Can't we do something? Couldn't <u>we</u> go and let him out?
Narrator 2	You know we can't do that. The only one that can help him now is his God!
Narrator 1	I've brought a box of tissues just in case!

Song 8   **JUST A BREATH AWAY**

During song Daniel goes and sits in a corner with his head bowed.

Narrator 1	He's so brave!
Narrator 2	I know. If I could get hold of those governors now...

Suddenly lions and trainers enter noisily.

Nora	OK guys. This is the big one. This is your Superbowl!
Nibbler	It'll make a change from an empty bowl!
Annie	Let's try some formations. First 'the antelope'.

Lions all get into tableau as though attacking an antelope.

Nora	Excellent. Now 'the wildebeest'. *(Another tableau)*
Annie	Perfect. I think they're ready Nora.
Nora	OK. Let's try 'the human!'

The lions pose then sniff and eventually spot Daniel and move threateningly towards him.

Annie	Let's just leave 'em to it!
Nora	See you later guys!

Annie and Nora exit. The lions are creeping towards Daniel when angels appear. Lions freeze.

Angel 1	*(In very soft voice)* Nice lions, sleepy lions!
Angels	*(Gently and rhythmically)* King of the beasts, it's <u>not</u> time to eat! Just close your <u>big</u> jaws up tight! King of the beasts, your <u>roaring</u> must cease Do <u>not</u> take a lick or a bite!

Lions freeze

Daniel	Who… Who are you?
Angel 1	We've been sent by the Lord God to watch over you and keep you safe.
Angel 2	So you just lie down and grab forty winks. We'll keep this lot occupied.

Daniel lies down. During the following, the lions settle down to sleep.

Angels	King of the beasts it's time now to sleep, Rock a bye kitties, good night! King of the beasts, your <u>hunger</u> will keep, Sleepy bye kitties, sleep tight!
Angel 1	Well done team! *(Looking at watch)* Oh! Nearly morning. Time we were off.

They tiptoe off. Governors enter, one carrying a doggie bag.

Governor 2	Poor Daniel! I bet he's not half the man he was.
Governor 3	Shame he won't be able to come to the banquet tonight. He hasn't got <u>any</u> <u>body</u> to go with! *(They all laugh)*
Governor 1	What's that you've got?
Governor 4	It's a doggie bag - for my doggies. There might be some leftovers!
Governors	<u>Urgh</u>*!*
Governor 4	Waste not, want not, I say.

Enter Darius and courtiers.

Darius	*(Shouting towards den)* Daniel! Daniel are you all right? Answer me, please!
Daniel	I'm fine! God sent his angels to keep me safe!
Governors	His what?!!

Guards mime unlocking door.

Darius	*(Shaking Daniel's hand energetically)* I can't believe it! You look better than ever!
Girl	Ooh! He does!

Governor 1	You mean after all our planning, he's survived? Why I'll... *(Other governors hold him back)*
Darius	So! This was all your doing! Well, I'm pleased to tell you that because of Daniel's God, those lions didn't even get a lick! *(All cheer)*

Song 9   **DID THE LIONS TAKE A BITE?**

Enter Annie and Nora.

Nora	Excuse me! I know you're all very thrilled that this chap is still alive and that's all very well, but what about our lions? They're still hungry! We may have to get animal welfare onto you!
Darius	I think I've got just the solution! *(Governors try to slope off)* Hey, you lot! You've got ten seconds' head start and then we're letting these fine beasts loose!
Governor 2	But your Compassionateness...!
Darius	*(Perhaps getting audience to join in – or Narrators)* 10,9,8 *etc.*

Governors run off and on 'Go!' lions chase them around hall/stage and off.

Governors	I want my mummy!/I'm innocent/He tastes better than me, *etc*!
Darius	Daniel, I think your God must be quite something! The next law I pass will say that everyone in Babylon has to worship Him and only Him! I can't think of any other god that could have rescued you from the lions.
Daniel	Good choice, King Darius. He is rather unique.
Girl	Your Majesty, I was just wondering, should we get rid of all the food and stuff the governors had ordered for the banquet tonight?
Darius	I don't know if a banquet is quite the thing for the moment...
Narrator 1	Of course it is! I'm starving!
Narrator 2	Party! Party! If this isn't a good reason for a celebration, I don't know what is!
Darius	Oh why not! A celebration in honour of the God of Daniel... The real King of the beasts!
Daniel	King of the whole world! Hey! I think there are some dancers who might like to join in. Shame to waste a good routine!

Song 10   **O WHAT A GREAT WONDER**

During song dancers do routine with Daniel.

Wanna Go Back

Words and Music by
Margaret Carpenter

16

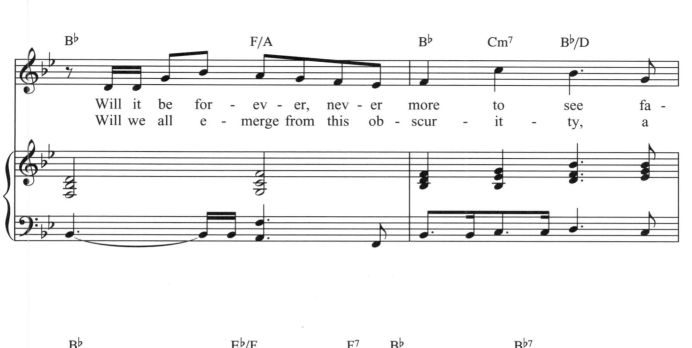

Will it be for - ev - er, nev - er more to see fa -
Will we all e - merge from this ob - scur - it - ty, a

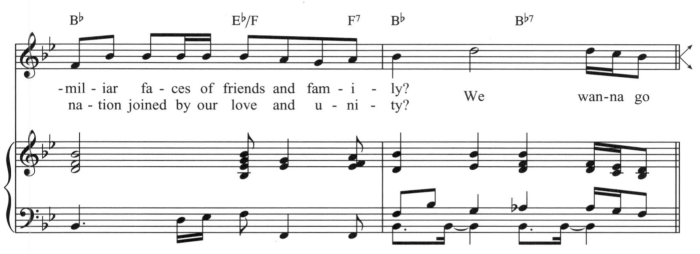

-mil - iar fa - ces of friends and fam - i - ly? We wan-na go
na - tion joined by our love and u - ni - ty?

back to our home - land, to the pla - ces that we know. Wan-na go

Wan-na go back, wan-na go back to pla - ces that we know.

back   to our home - land   where the milk and hon-ey flow.___ Wan-na go

Wan-na go back,   wan-na go   back where the milk and   hon-ey   flow.___

back   to our home - land,   to the land of li-ber - ty;___   wan-na go

Wan-na go back,   wan-na go   back;   we want   li-ber - ty.___

1.

back,   wan-na go back,   wan-na go   back   and   be free!

Wan-na go   back,   wan-na go   back,   wan-na go and   be free!

18

Babylon

Words and Music by
Margaret Carpenter

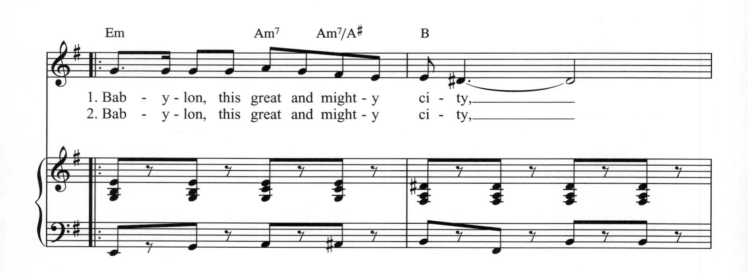

1. Bab - y - lon, this great and might - y ci - ty,_____
2. Bab - y - lon, this great and might - y ci - ty,_____

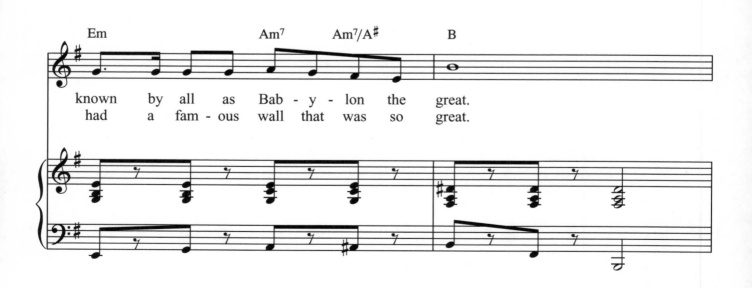

known by all as Bab - y - lon the great.
had a fam - ous wall that was so great.

Full of wealth and pow - er, rich bey - ond com - pare.
Char - i - ots a - plent - y, two by two could go;

Fam - ous hang - ing gar - dens were all there.
peo - ple gazed in won - der from be - low.

Dar - i - us the King, a - mong the might - y
Dar - i - us the Mede he had great pow - er,

ruled the land with pow - er and great fear.
his the hand that signed the new de - crees.

21

His, the land of plen-ty,
flow - er of the East.
Laws of Medes and Pers-ians
had to be o-beyed;

An - y who'd op-pose him take care.
pun-ish-ment was nev-er de-layed.
But you can

eat our sump-tuous food, no-one is ex-clud-ed; we've

man-y gods,__ so bow to them all.

22

How Do You Do It?

Words and Music by
Margaret Carpenter

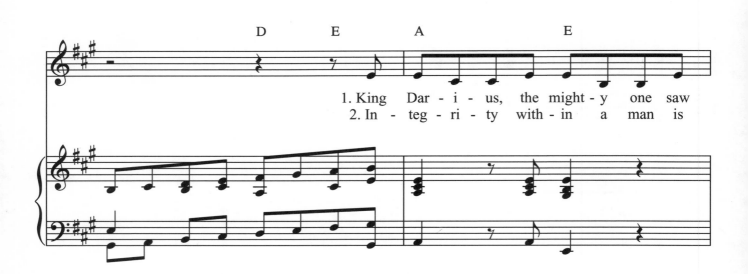

1. King Dar - i - us, the might - y one saw
2. In - teg - ri - ty with - in a man is

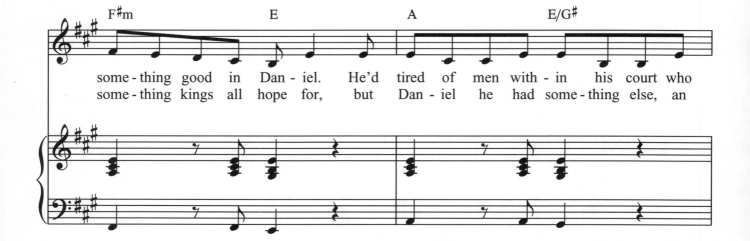

some - thing good in Dan - iel. He'd tired of men with - in his court who
some - thing kings all hope for, but Dan - iel he had some - thing else, an

must be much more to it. Dan - iel, Dan - iel

how do you do it? It is - n't just that hon - est face, there

1.
must be much more to it.

2.
must be

much more to it!

4

So Stuck Up

Words and Music by
Margaret Carpenter

1. Look at that Dan - iel ov - er___ there! He's so stuck up with his nose in the air,___ and
2. Look at that Dan - iel ov - er___ there! We want him gone and we real - ly don't care, 'cos

now that the King thinks he's one of the best;___ is
now that the King thinks he's one of the best;___ won't

just the rea - son we de - test that Dan - iel,_
stop us in our ev - il quest with

Dan - iel;_ he'd bet - ter not turn_ his back. 'Cos

Dan - iel,_ that Dan - iel man; we're gon - na get, gon - na

bad be - hav - iour.

Be just a lit - tle bit

bad,

we'd be so

glad!

glad!

Look at that Dan - iel ov - er there!

5

Jealousy And Hatred

Words and Music by
Margaret Carpenter

Kneel

With stealth (♩ = 83)

1. Jea - lous-y and hat - red don't be - long in your heart.
2. Jea - lous-y and hat - red, they will grip you so tight.

We will get a grip, then sure - ly tear you a - part.
Ev - en if you strug - gle they will still win the fight.

Don't in - vite them, or en - tice them, close that door.
Don't be tempt - ed by their e - vil, strange ap - peal.

We'll im-press you, then pos-sess you more and more.
An-y scrap of good in-ten - tions they will steal.

Don't let that poi - son pol - lute your mind,

or you will slow - ly find that it has

ta - ken you o - ver in mind and soul,

6 Learn verse 2

Let's Trap Him

Words and Music by
Margaret Carpenter

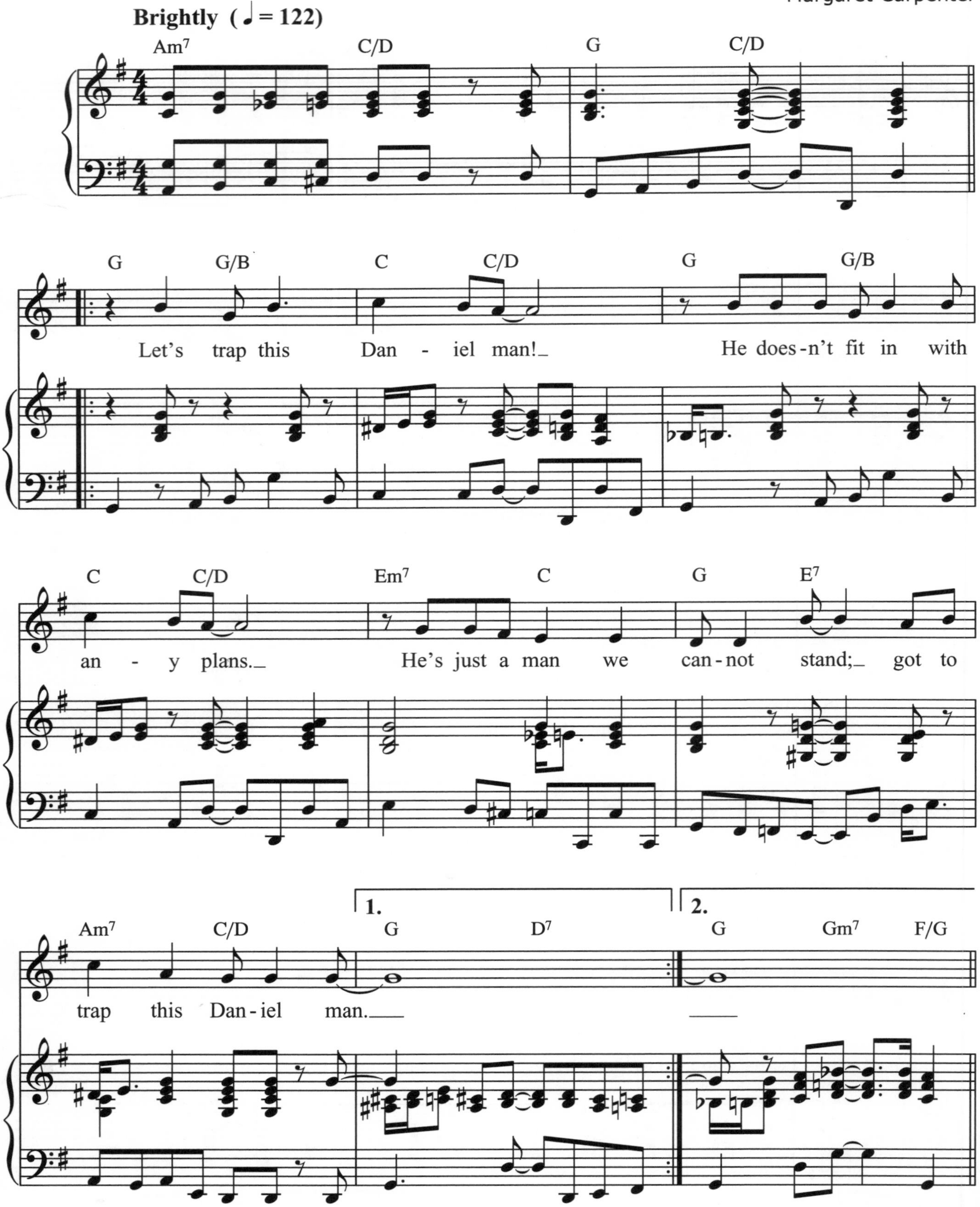

Brightly (♩ = 122)
Am7 C/D G C/D
G G/B C C/D G G/B
Let's trap this Dan - iel man! He does-n't fit in with
C C/D Em7 C G E7
an - y plans. He's just a man we can-not stand; got to
Am7 C/D 1. G D7 2. G Gm7 F/G
trap this Dan-iel man.

1. What a good-y good-y is this___ Dan-iel bloke!
2. Could we get the King to make a___ new de-cree?

We would like to trap him, it would___ be a joke.
Prayer re-quest were on-ly to his___ ma-jes-ty. Would

Take him down a peg or two to be like the rest,___
Dan-iel keep on pray-ing to his God up a-bove?_

we must find a way to put his faith to the test.___ Well,
What a good ex-cuse to give this Dan-iel the shove!_

Let's trap this Dan - iel man!_ He does-n't fit in with

an - y plans._ He's just a man we can-not stand;_ got to

1. trap this Dan-iel man.___ **2.**

CODA

trap this Dan - iel man!___

verse 2

Keep On Trusting

Words and Music by
Margaret Carpenter

Keep on trust-ing, keep on trust-ing, keep on trust-ing Dan-iel man._

1. Dan-iel was so ve-ry strong, and he knew the King's law it was
2. Dan-iel, he was not a-fraid_ just to keep on pray-ing three

ve-ry wrong._ Not a-fraid of trou-ble if he
times a day.___ No-thing they could do would make him

did-n't kneel;_ 'cos the King's e - dict had no ap - peal._
change his mind,_ 'cos he knew his God was the jea-lous kind._

See his faith grow-ing day af-ter day; all he had to do was

kneel down and pray to the God a - bove,_ "Help me not give in!"_

All he had to do was put his trust in Him___ and the

Just A Breath Away

Words and Music by
Margaret Carpenter

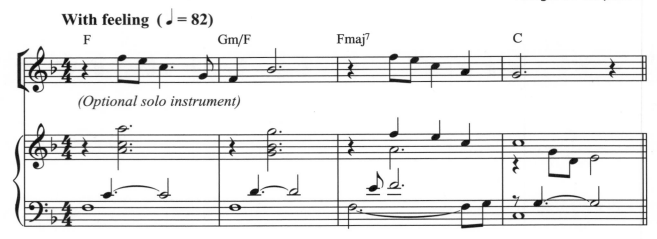

(Optional solo instrument)

1. Sud - den - ly_____ I'm so a - lone,_____ and fear is all a - round me.

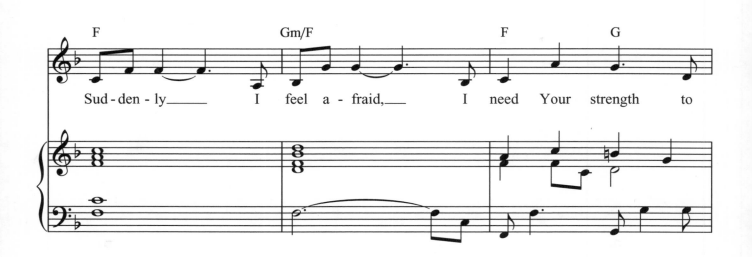

Sud - den - ly_____ I feel a - fraid,_____ I need Your strength to

help me see that You are just a breath a - way, that You will

help me face this day. I know You'll hear me when I

pray; You're faith - ful_ and true and I'll face_ the fu - ture

now with You.

(Optional solo instrument)

Did The Lions Take A Bite?

Words and Music by
Margaret Carpenter

snug - gled,___ snug - gled___ down___ at Dan - iel's___ feet.___

2. Did the

2. Well, did Dan - iel start to fret? Did he

* If you wish to play along in this section, please use the chords for verse 3, bars 77 – 107.

O What A Great Wonder

Words and Music by
Margaret Carpenter

1. I rule a great king - dom with pow - er and fame.
2. I rule a great king - dom with vig - our and sway.

Cap - tives are a - plen - ty but one day there came a
I sign the de - crees and the peo - ple o - bey. But

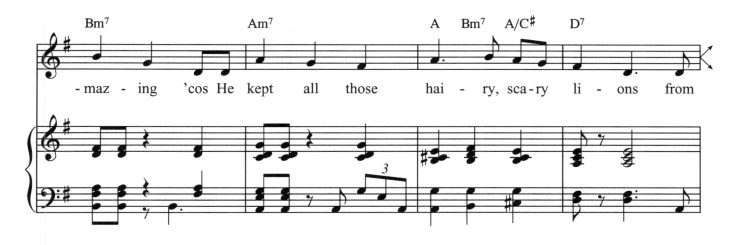

-maz - ing 'cos He kept all those hai - ry, sca - ry li - ons from

tak - ing one bite._____ O what a great

O what a

won - der! Dan - iel was right. His God is a -

won - der, that Dan - iel was right. An - gels were

Wanna Go Back

Track 1:   full version
Track 11:   backing track

Wanna go back, wanna go back,
Wanna go back, wanna go back.

1
Here we are as captives in a distant land,
It's a very sad and lonely place.
Will it be forever, never more to see
Familiar faces of friends and family?

Chorus
(See music score
for harmony lyrics)

We wanna go back to our homeland,
To the places that we know.
Wanna go back to our homeland,
Where the milk and honey flow.
Wanna go back to our homeland,
To the land of liberty;
Wanna go back, wanna go back,
Wanna go back and be free!

2
Will our Lord Jehovah still be with us here,
In this foreign land and unknown place?
Will we all emerge from this obscurity,
A nation joined by our love and unity?

Chorus
(See music score
for harmony lyrics)

We wanna go back to our homeland,
To the places that we know.
Wanna go back to our homeland,
Where the milk and honey flow.
Wanna go back to our homeland,
To the land of liberty;
Wanna go back, wanna go back,
Wanna go back home and be free!
We wanna be free!

Babylon

Track 2:   full version
Track 12:   backing track

1   Babylon, this great and mighty city,
         Known by all as Babylon the great.
         Full of wealth and power, rich beyond compare.
         Famous hanging gardens were all there.
         Darius the King, among the mighty
         Ruled the land with power and great fear.
         His, the land of plenty, flower of the East.
         Any who'd oppose him take care.

Chorus   *But you can eat our sumptuous food,*
         No-one is excluded;
         We've many gods, so bow to them all.
         You will feel at home in this land of plenty,
         But make sure that you just don't fall, yes!

2   Babylon, this great and mighty city,
         Had a famous wall that was so great.
         Chariots aplenty, two by two could go;
         People gazed in wonder from below.
         Darius the Mede he had great power,
         His the hand that signed the new decrees.
         Laws of Medes and Persians had to be obeyed;
         Punishment was never delayed.

Chorus   *But you can eat our sumptuous food,*
         No-one is excluded;
         We've many gods, so bow to them all.
         You will feel at home in this land of plenty,
         In this land of the East, let your eyes feast
         On Babylon the great.

How Do You Do It?

Track 3:   full version
Track 13:   backing track

1   King Darius, the mighty one
     Saw something good in Daniel.
     He'd tired of men within his court
     Who gave him lots of flannel.
     An honest man was something new,
     A good hard worker too.
     He'd give this man some extra power;
     Yes that's what he would do.

Chorus   *Daniel, Daniel how do you do it?*
          It isn't just that honest face,
          There must be much more to it.
          Daniel, Daniel how do you do it?
          It isn't just that honest face,
          There must be much more to it.

2   Integrity within a man
     Is something kings all hope for,
     But Daniel he had something else,
     An inner peace and what's more,
     An honest man was something new,
     A good hard worker too.
     He'd give this man some extra power;
     Yes that's what he would do.

Chorus   *Daniel, Daniel how do you do it?*
          It isn't just that honest face,
          There must be much more to it.
          Daniel, Daniel how do you do it?
          It isn't just that honest face,
          There must be much more to it.

So Stuck Up

Track 4:   full version
Track 14:   backing track

1   Look at that Daniel over there!
He's so stuck up with his nose in the air,
And now that the King thinks he's one of the best;
Is just the reason we detest that Daniel, Daniel;
He'd better not turn his back.
'Cos Daniel, that Daniel man;
We're gonna get, gonna get him the sack.

Chorus   *'Cos we know he's the King's own pickin',*
It really makes us sick, yuk!
How much would it cost to tempt him
Out of favour to be a raver,
Show some very bad behaviour?
Be just a little be bad,
We'd be so glad!

2   Look at that Daniel over there!
We want him gone and we really don't care,
'Cos now that the King thinks he's one of the best;
Won't stop us in our evil quest with Daniel, Daniel;
He'd better not turn his back.
'Cos Daniel, that Daniel man;
We're gonna get, gonna get him the sack.

Chorus   *'Cos we know he's the King's own pickin',*
It really makes us sick, yuk!
How much would it cost to tempt him
Out of favour to be a raver,
Show some very bad behaviour?
Be just a little bit bad,
We'd be so glad!

Look at that Daniel over there!

Jealousy And Hatred

Track 5:   full version
Track 15:   backing track

1
Jealousy and hatred don't belong in your heart.
We will get a grip, then surely tear you apart.
Don't invite them, or entice them, close that door.
We'll impress you, then possess you more and more.

Chorus
Don't let that poison pollute your mind,
Or you will slowly find that it has
Taken you over in mind and soul,
And then you'll lose control.

2
Jealousy and hatred, they will grip you so tight.
Even if you struggle they will still win the fight.
Don't be tempted by their evil, strange appeal.
Any scrap of good intentions they will steal.

Chorus
Don't let that poison pollute your mind,
Or you will slowly find that it has
Taken you over in mind and soul,
And then you'll lose control; don't let that,
Don't let that poison pollute your mind.
You're sure to lose your self-control.

Let's Trap Him

Track 6:   full version
Track 16:   backing track

Chorus

Let's trap this Daniel man!
He doesn't fit in with any plans.
He's just a man we cannot stand;
Got to trap this Daniel man.
Let's trap this Daniel man!
He doesn't fit in with any plans.
He's just a man we cannot stand;
Got to trap this Daniel man.

1

What a goody, goody is this Daniel bloke!
We would like to trap him, it would be a joke.
Take him down a peg or two to be like the rest,
We must find a way to put his faith to the test. Well...

Chorus

Let's trap this Daniel man!
He doesn't fit in with any plans.
He's just a man we cannot stand;
Got to trap this Daniel man.

2

Could we get the King to make a new decree?
Prayer requests were only to his Majesty.
Would Daniel keep on praying to his God up above?
What a good excuse to give this Daniel the shove!

Chorus

Let's trap this Daniel man!
He doesn't fit in with any plans.
He's just a man we cannot stand;
Got to trap this Daniel man.
Let's trap this Daniel man!
He doesn't fit in with any plans.
He's just a man we cannot stand;
Got to trap this Daniel man!

Keep On Trusting

Track 7: full version
Track 17: backing track

Keep on trusting, keep on trusting,
Keep on trusting Daniel man.

1
Daniel was so very strong,
And he knew the King's law it was very wrong.
Not afraid of trouble if he didn't kneel;
'Cos the King's edict had no appeal.

Chorus
See his faith growing day after day;
All he had to do was kneel down and pray
To the God above, "Help me not give in!"
All he had to do was put his trust in Him
And the God above kept him free from sin,
As Daniel put his trust in Him.
(Keep on trusting, keep on trusting,
Keep on trusting Daniel man.)

2
Daniel, he was not afraid
Just to keep on praying three times a day.
Nothing they could do would make him change his mind,
'Cos he knew his God was the jealous kind.

Chorus
See his faith growing day after day;
All he had to do was kneel down and pray
To the God above, "Help me not give in!"
All he had to do was put his trust in Him
And the God above kept him free from sin,
As Daniel put his trust in Him.
(Keep on trusting, keep on trusting,
Keep on trusting Daniel man.)

Just A Breath Away

Track 8:   full version
Track 18:   backing track

1

(Daniel)
Suddenly I'm so alone,
And fear is all around me.
Suddenly I feel afraid,
I need Your strength to help me see
That You are just a breath away,
That You will help me face this day.
I know You'll hear me when I pray;
You're faithful and true
And I'll face the future now with You.

2

(Daniel)
Suddenly I'm so alone
And fear is all
Around me.
Suddenly I feel afraid,
I need Your strength
To help me see
That You are just a breath away,
That You will help me face this day.
I know You'll hear me when I pray.
You're faithful and true
And I'll face the future there
With You

(Darius)
O Daniel
What have I done,
What have I done to you now?
O Daniel
What a mistake,
I realise now
that my foolish pride
Had blinded my eyes
Now what can I say?
I just hope
Your God will be there
Today.

Did The Lions Take A Bite?

Track 9:   full version
Track 19:   backing track

1   Did the lions take a bite out of Daniel in the night?
    No, they didn't!
    And did Daniel have to fight with his power and his might?
    No, he didn't!
    In the middle of that dangerous scene
    A superpower stopped the lions feeling mean, mean, mean;
    They just snuggled, snuggled down at Daniel's feet.

2   Did the lions even scowl, give a tiny little growl?
    No, they didn't!
    Did they even start to prowl, causing Dan to give a howl?
    No, they didn't!
    In the middle of that dangerous scene
    A superpower stopped the lions feeling mean, mean, mean;
    They just snuggled, snuggled down at Daniel's feet.

    Instrumental

3   Well, did Daniel start to fret? Did he break into a sweat?
    No, he didn't!
    Did he even get upset? You can make your biggest bet
    That he didn't!
    In the middle of that dangerous scene
    A superpower stopped the lions feeling mean, mean, mean;
    They just snuggled, snuggled down at Daniel's feet.

O What A Great Wonder

Track 10:   full version
Track 20:   backing track

1
I rule a great kingdom with power and fame.
Captives are aplenty but one day there came
A young man called Daniel who rose to the heights,
Which gave him some clout, made him stand out,
There was no doubt he was bright.

Chorus
O what a great wonder!
Daniel was right.
His God is amazing
'Cos He kept all those hairy, scary lions
From taking one bite.   *(Harmony)*
O what a great wonder!   *O what a wonder, that*
Daniel was right.   *Daniel was right.*
His God is amazing   *Angels were keeping*
'Cos He kept all those hairy, scary lions *Those big scary lions*
From taking one bite.   *From taking one bite.*

2
I rule a great kingdom with vigour and sway.
I sign the decrees and the people obey.
But one day because my advisors had lied,
I signed a decree honouring me,
So foolishly in my pride.

Chorus
O what a great wonder!
Daniel was right.
His God is amazing
'Cos He kept all those hairy, scary lions
From taking one bite.   *(Harmony)*
O what a great wonder!   *O what a wonder, that*
Daniel was right.   *Daniel was right.*
His God is amazing   *Angels were keeping*
'Cos He kept all those hairy, scary lions *Those big scary lions*
From taking one bite.   *From taking one bite.*

(UK / EIRE / EU) LICENCE APPLICATION FORM

To stage this play in non-EU countries please contact Out of the Ark Music for an alternative form.

If you perform **Daniel – A Hard Act To Swallow** to an audience other than children and staff you will need to photocopy and complete this form and return it by post or fax to Out of the Ark Music in order to apply for a licence. *If anticipated audience sizes are very small or if special circumstances apply please contact us.*

We wish to apply for a licence to perform 'Daniel' by Margaret Carpenter

Customer number (if known): ....

Name of school / organisation: ....

Name of organiser / producer: ....

Date(s) of performance(s): ....

Invoice address: ....

....

Post code: .... **Country:** ....

Telephone number: ....

Number of performances (excl. dress rehearsal)	Performances without admission charges	Performances with admission charges
1	☐ £11.75* (inc VAT)	☐ £18.80* (inc VAT)
2	☐ £18.80* (inc VAT)	☐ £23.50* (inc VAT)

Tick one of the boxes above. For 3 or more performances contact Out of the Ark Music for details.

Tick one of the three payment options below: *(Invoices will be sent with all licences)*

☐ Please bill me / my school or nursery at the above address

☐ I enclose a cheque (pounds sterling) for £   payable to **Out of the Ark Music**

☐ Please charge the following card: (VISA, MasterCard and American Express accepted)

Card no:	Start date: __/__ (MM/YY)	Expiry date: __/__ (MM/YY)	3 digit security code: _ _ _ (last 3 digits on signature strip)

If the performance is to be recorded in order to sell the recording to parents or to the public please contact Out of the Ark Music. We convey to the licence holder the right to reproduce printed lyrics of the songs in programmes distributed to the audience. The following credit should be included with the lyrics: *'Reproduced by kind permission. © Out of the Ark Music'*

Address: Out of the Ark Music
Sefton House
2 Molesey Road
Hersham Green
Walton-on-Thames
Surrey KT12 4RQ
United Kingdom

Phone: +44 (0)1932 232 250
Fax: +44 (0)1932 703 010
Email: info@outoftheark.com

*The licence fees shown on this form are for 2004–2005 and may be subject to revision.

Christmas Musicals
By Mark & Helen Johnson

4-9s

it's a cracker!

5 - 9s

Another fantastic nativity musical by Mark and Helen Johnson

Each songbook package provides:

Quality recordings of all the songs, sung by children

Professionally arranged and produced backing tracks

Piano music with melody, lyrics and guitar chords

Photocopiable lyric sheets

it's a party!

Key Stages 1 and 2

A great new nativity musical by Mark and Helen Johnson

it's a cracker!

A great new musical that mixes the Christmas dinner festivities with the awe and wonder of the Nativity story. Nine great songs everyone will love.

* Age: 5-9s
* Cast size: 25 upwards
* Speaking parts: 22
* Duration: c. 40 mins

it's a baby!

Nursery and Infants

9 new nativity songs for 3-7 year olds by Mark and Helen Johnson

it's a party

The invitations were unusual... the guest were unlikely... and the venue wa unconventional – but what a party! With great new songs, party on and celebrate i style with this brilliant nativity musical

Age: 5-9s
Cast size: 24 upwards
Speaking parts: minimum 16
Duration: c. 30 mins

are we nearly there yet...?

5-9's

Another great nativity musical by Mark and Helen Johnson

it's a baby!

The Christmas story, but with a difference! Told from the perspective of a weary innkeeper who finds he's in for a sleepless night...

Perfectly suited to younger voices, the 9 new songs are funny, melodic and very singable – guaranteed to have immediate appeal! Simple rhyming narrative links and percussion parts are provided.

* Age: 4-7s
* Cast size: 12 upwards
* Speaking parts: minimum 3
* Duration: c. 30 mins

off to bethlehem

5 - 9s

9 original nativity songs by Mark and Helen Johnson

are we nearly there yet?

Everyone's preparing to make the journey to Bethlehem. Whilst Mary and Joseph, the shepherds and the angels set off, we join the Walker family on their journey. You will smile as they encounter the trials and tribulations that make up a typical family outing.

* Age: 5-9s
* Cast size: 18 upwards
Speaking parts: minimum 18 *
Duration: c. 35 mins *

off to bethlehem

9 delightful songs present the traditional Christmas stor without the need for lengthy narration or dialogu

Everything you need for a superb production provided in this comprehensive packag

*Age: 5-9s *Cast size: 21 upwards *Duration: c. 30 min

Out of the Ark Music, Sefton House, 2 Molesey Road, Hersham Green, Surrey KT12 4RQ
Telephone 01932 232250, Fax 01932 703010
Email info@outoftheark.com, www.outoftheark.com

Out of the Ark Music